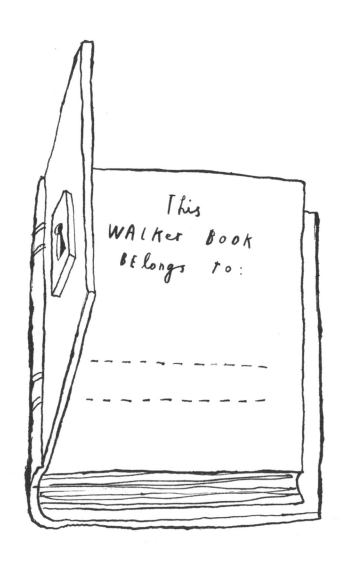

This
WALKer BOOK
BElongs To:

- - - - - - - - - -

- - - - - - - - - -

The Golden Goose *as told by Jacob Grimm and Wilhelm Grimm,* Tom Thumb *as told by Richard Johnson,* The Golden Bird *as told by Jacob Grimm and Wilhelm Grimm,* Snow White and Rose Red *as told by Jacob Grimm and Wi*
by Bram Stoker ∽ THE ROPE ∽ Rapunzel *as told by Jacob Grimm and Wilhelm Grimm* ∽ THE CLOUDS ∽ Suo Gân *as adapted by Robert Bryan,* Twinkle, Twinkle, Little Star *by Jane Taylor,* Hush-a-Bye Baby *as adapted by J*
ay Alcott, The Three Musketeers *by Alexandre Dumas,* The Tale of Peter Rabbit *by Beatrix Potter,* Alice's Adventures in Wonderland *by Lewis Carroll,* Great Expectations *by Charles Dickens,* Adventures of Huckleberry Finn *b*
Malory and Sir James Knowles and Rip Van Winkle *by Washington Irving* ∽ THE SEA ∽ The Voyages of Doctor Dolittle *by Hugh Lofting,* The Swiss Family Robinson *by Johann David Wyss,* Robinson Crusoe *by Daniel Defoe,*
n Crusoe *by Daniel Defoe,* The Swiss Family Robinson *by Johann David Wyss,* The Adventures of Pinocchio *by Carlo Collodi* and Twenty Thousand Leagues Under the Sea *by Jules Verne* ∽ THE HOLE ∽ Alice's Adventures
mm and Wilhelm Grimm, Hansel & Gretel *as told by Jacob Grimm and Wilhelm Grimm,* The Golden Goose *as told by Jacob Grimm and Wilhelm Grimm,* Tom Thumb *as told by Richard Johnson,* The Golden Bird *as told by Jacob*
end of Sleepy Hollow *by Washington Irving,* Frankenstein *by Mary Shelley* and Dracula *by Bram Stoker* ∽ THE ROPE ∽ Rapunzel *as told by Jacob Grimm and Wilhelm Grimm* ∽ THE CLOUDS ∽ Suo Gân *as adapted by Robe*
nk Baum, The Wind in the Willows *by Kenneth Grahame,* Little Women *by Louisa May Alcott,* The Three Musketeers *by Alexandre Dumas,* The Tale of Peter Rabbit *by Beatrix Potter,* Alice's Adventures in Wonderland *by Lew*
auty *by Anna Sewell,* The Legends of King Arthur and His Knights *by Sir Thomas Malory and Sir James Knowles* and Rip Van Winkle *by Washington Irving* ∽ THE SEA ∽ The Voyages of Doctor Dolittle *by Hugh Lofting,* Th
e Sea *by Jules Verne* ∽ THE WAVE ∽ Gulliver's Travels *by Jonathan Swift,* Robinson Crusoe *by Daniel Defoe,* The Swiss Family Robinson *by Johann David Wyss,* The Adventures of Pinocchio *by Carlo Collodi* and Twenty Th
ed *by Robert Louis Stevenson* ∽ THE FOREST ∽ Little Red Cap *as told by Jacob Grimm and Wilhelm Grimm,* Hansel & Gretel *as told by Jacob Grimm and Wilhelm Grimm,* The Golden Goose *as told by Jacob Grimm and Wilhe*
unzel *as told by Jacob Grimm and Wilhelm Grimm* ∽ THE MONSTER ∽ The Legend of Sleepy Hollow *by Washington Irving,* Frankenstein *by Mary Shelley* and Dracula *by Bram Stoker* ∽ THE ROPE ∽ Rapunzel *as told by Ja*
the Moon *by Jules Verne* ∽ THE WORLD ∽ The Wonderful Wizard of Oz *by L. Frank Baum,* The Wind in the Willows *by Kenneth Grahame,* Little Women *by Louisa May Alcott,* The Three Musketeers *by Alexandre Dumas,* T
The Secret Garden *by Frances Hodgson Burnett,* Heidi *by Johanna Spyri,* Black Beauty *by Anna Sewell,* The Legends of King Arthur and His Knights *by Sir Thomas Malory and Sir James Knowles* and Rip Van Winkle *by Washin*
, Gulliver's Travels *by Jonathan Swift* and Twenty Thousand Leagues Under the Sea *by Jules Verne* ∽ THE WAVE ∽ Gulliver's Travels *by Jonathan Swift,* Robinson Crusoe *by Daniel Defoe,* The Swiss Family Robinson *by Joh*
rie ∽ THE CAVE ∽ Treasure Island *by Robert Louis Stevenson* and Kidnapped *by Robert Louis Stevenson* ∽ THE FOREST ∽ Little Red Cap *as told by Jacob Grimm and Wilhelm Grimm,* Hansel & Gretel *as told by Jacob Grim*
Grimm, Beauty and the Beast *by Jeanne-Marie Leprince de Beaumont* and Rapunzel *as told by Jacob Grimm and Wilhelm Grimm* ∽ THE MONSTER ∽ The Legend of Sleepy Hollow *by Washington Irving,* Frankenstein *by Ma*
bery and Brahms' Lullaby *by Johannes Brahms* ∽ THE MOON ∽ Around the Moon *by Jules Verne* ∽ THE WORLD ∽ The Wonderful Wizard of Oz *by L. Frank Baum,* The Wind in the Willows *by Kenneth Grahame,* Little
ain, A Christmas Carol *by Charles Dickens,* Moby Dick *by Herman Melville,* The Secret Garden *by Frances Hodgson Burnett,* Heidi *by Johanna Spyri,* Black Beauty *by Anna Sewell,* The Legends of King Arthur and His Knight
f Monte Cristo *by Alexandre Dumas,* Kidnapped *by Robert Louis Stevenson,* Gulliver's Travels *by Jonathan Swift* and Twenty Thousand Leagues Under the Sea *by Jules Verne* ∽ THE WAVE ∽ Gulliver's Travels *by Jonathan Swi*
and *by Lewis Carroll* ∽ THE MOUNTAINS ∽ Peter Pan and Wendy *by J.M. Barrie* ∽ THE CAVE ∽ Treasure Island *by Robert Louis Stevenson* and Kidnapped *by Robert Louis Stevenson* ∽ THE FOREST ∽ Little Red Cap *a*
nd Wilhelm Grimm, Snow White and Rose Red *as told by Jacob Grimm and Wilhelm Grimm,* Beauty and the Beast *by Jeanne-Marie Leprince de Beaumont* and Rapunzel *as told by Jacob Grimm and Wilhelm Grimm* ∽ THE MO
winkle, Twinkle, Little Star *by Jane Taylor,* Hush-a-Bye Baby *as adapted by John Newbery* and Brahms' Lullaby *by Johannes Brahms* ∽ THE MOON ∽ Around the Moon *by Jules Verne* ∽ THE WORLD ∽ The Wonderful Wi
Great Expectations *by Charles Dickens,* Adventures of Huckleberry Finn *by Mark Twain,* A Christmas Carol *by Charles Dickens,* Moby Dick *by Herman Melville,* The Secret Garden *by Frances Hodgson Burnett,* Heidi *by Johann*
mily Robinson *by Johann David Wyss,* Robinson Crusoe *by Daniel Defoe,* The Count of Monte Cristo *by Alexandre Dumas,* Kidnapped *by Robert Louis Stevenson,* Gulliver's Travels *by Jonathan Swift* and Twenty Thousand Lea
Under the Sea *by Jules Verne* ∽ THE HOLE ∽ Alice's Adventures in Wonderland *by Lewis Carroll* ∽ THE MOUNTAINS ∽ Peter Pan and Wendy *by J.M. Barrie* ∽ THE CAVE ∽ Treasure Island *by Robert Louis Stevenson a*
umb *as told by Richard Johnson,* The Golden Bird *as told by Jacob Grimm and Wilhelm Grimm,* Snow White and Rose Red *as told by Jacob Grimm and Wilhelm Grimm,* Beauty and the Beast *by Jeanne-Marie Leprince de Beaumon*
elm Grimm ∽ THE CLOUDS ∽ Suo Gân *as adapted by Robert Bryan,* Twinkle, Twinkle, Little Star *by Jane Taylor,* Hush-a-Bye Baby *as adapted by John Newbery* and Brahms' Lullaby *by Johannes Brahms* ∽ THE MOON ∽ A
bbit *by Beatrix Potter,* Alice's Adventures in Wonderland *by Lewis Carroll,* Great Expectations *by Charles Dickens,* Adventures of Huckleberry Finn *by Mark Twain,* A Christmas Carol *by Charles Dickens,* Moby Dick *by Herm*
SEA ∽ The Voyages of Doctor Dolittle *by Hugh Lofting,* The Swiss Family Robinson *by Johann David Wyss,* Robinson Crusoe *by Daniel Defoe,* The Count of Monte Cristo *by Alexandre Dumas,* Kidnapped *by Robert Louis St*
entures of Pinocchio *by Carlo Collodi* and Twenty Thousand Leagues Under the Sea *by Jules Verne* ∽ THE HOLE ∽ Alice's Adventures in Wonderland *by Lewis Carroll* ∽ THE MOUNTAINS ∽ Peter Pan and Wendy *by J.*
The Golden Goose *as told by Jacob Grimm and Wilhelm Grimm,* Tom Thumb *as told by Richard Johnson,* The Golden Bird *as told by Jacob Grimm and Wilhelm Grimm,* Snow White and Rose Red *as told by Jacob Grimm and Wil*
by Bram Stoker ∽ THE ROPE ∽ Rapunzel *as told by Jacob Grimm and Wilhelm Grimm* ∽ THE CLOUDS ∽ Suo Gân *as adapted by Robert Bryan,* Twinkle, Twinkle, Little Star *by Jane Taylor,* Hush-a-Bye Baby *as adapted by J*
ay Alcott, The Three Musketeers *by Alexandre Dumas,* The Tale of Peter Rabbit *by Beatrix Potter,* Alice's Adventures in Wonderland *by Lewis Carroll,* Great Expectations *by Charles Dickens,* Adventures of Huckleberry Finn *b*
Malory and Sir James Knowles and Rip Van Winkle *by Washington Irving* ∽ THE SEA ∽ The Voyages of Doctor Dolittle *by Hugh Lofting,* The Swiss Family Robinson *by Johann David Wyss,* Robinson Crusoe *by Daniel Defoe,*
n Crusoe *by Daniel Defoe,* The Swiss Family Robinson *by Johann David Wyss,* The Adventures of Pinocchio *by Carlo Collodi* and Twenty Thousand Leagues Under the Sea *by Jules Verne* ∽ THE HOLE ∽ Alice's Adventures
mm and Wilhelm Grimm, Hansel & Gretel *as told by Jacob Grimm and Wilhelm Grimm,* The Golden Goose *as told by Jacob Grimm and Wilhelm Grimm,* Tom Thumb *as told by Richard Johnson,* The Golden Bird *as told by Jacob*
end of Sleepy Hollow *by Washington Irving,* Frankenstein *by Mary Shelley* and Dracula *by Bram Stoker* ∽ THE ROPE ∽ Rapunzel *as told by Jacob Grimm and Wilhelm Grimm* ∽ THE CLOUDS ∽ Suo Gân *as adapted by Robe*
nk Baum, The Wind in the Willows *by Kenneth Grahame,* Little Women *by Louisa May Alcott,* The Three Musketeers *by Alexandre Dumas,* The Tale of Peter Rabbit *by Beatrix Potter,* Alice's Adventures in Wonderland *by Lewi*
auty *by Anna Sewell,* The Legends of King Arthur and His Knights *by Sir Thomas Malory and Sir James Knowles* and Rip Van Winkle *by Washington Irving* ∽ THE SEA ∽ The Voyages of Doctor Dolittle *by Hugh Lofting,* Th
e Sea *by Jules Verne* ∽ THE WAVE ∽ Gulliver's Travels *by Jonathan Swift,* Robinson Crusoe *by Daniel Defoe,* The Swiss Family Robinson *by Johann David Wyss,* The Adventures of Pinocchio *by Carlo Collodi* and Twenty Th
ed *by Robert Louis Stevenson* ∽ THE FOREST ∽ Little Red Cap *as told by Jacob Grimm and Wilhelm Grimm,* Hansel & Gretel *as told by Jacob Grimm and Wilhelm Grimm,* The Golden Goose *as told by Jacob Grimm and Wilhe*
unzel *as told by Jacob Grimm and Wilhelm Grimm* ∽ THE MONSTER ∽ The Legend of Sleepy Hollow *by Washington Irving,* Frankenstein *by Mary Shelley* and Dracula *by Bram Stoker* ∽ THE ROPE ∽ Rapunzel *as told by Ja*
the Moon *by Jules Verne* ∽ THE WORLD ∽ The Wonderful Wizard of Oz *by L. Frank Baum,* The Wind in the Willows *by Kenneth Grahame,* Little Women *by Louisa May Alcott,* The Three Musketeers *by Alexandre Dumas,* T
The Secret Garden *by Frances Hodgson Burnett,* Heidi *by Johanna Spyri,* Black Beauty *by Anna Sewell,* The Legends of King Arthur and His Knights *by Sir Thomas Malory and Sir James Knowles* and Rip Van Winkle *by Washin*
, Gulliver's Travels *by Jonathan Swift* and Twenty Thousand Leagues Under the Sea *by Jules Verne* ∽ THE WAVE ∽ Gulliver's Travels *by Jonathan Swift,* Robinson Crusoe *by Daniel Defoe,* The Swiss Family Robinson *by Joh*
rie ∽ THE CAVE ∽ Treasure Island *by Robert Louis Stevenson* and Kidnapped *by Robert Louis Stevenson* ∽ THE FOREST ∽ Little Red Cap *as told by Jacob Grimm and Wilhelm Grimm,* Hansel & Gretel *as told by Jacob Grim*
Grimm, Beauty and the Beast *by Jeanne-Marie Leprince de Beaumont* and Rapunzel *as told by Jacob Grimm and Wilhelm Grimm* ∽ THE MONSTER ∽ The Legend of Sleepy Hollow *by Washington Irving,* Frankenstein *by Ma*
bery and Brahms' Lullaby *by Johannes Brahms* ∽ THE MOON ∽ Around the Moon *by Jules Verne* ∽ THE WORLD ∽ The Wonderful Wizard of Oz *by L. Frank Baum,* The Wind in the Willows *by Kenneth Grahame,* Little
ain, A Christmas Carol *by Charles Dickens,* Moby Dick *by Herman Melville,* The Secret Garden *by Frances Hodgson Burnett,* Heidi *by Johanna Spyri,* Black Beauty *by Anna Sewell,* The Legends of King Arthur and His Knight
f Monte Cristo *by Alexandre Dumas,* Kidnapped *by Robert Louis Stevenson,* Gulliver's Travels *by Jonathan Swift* and Twenty Thousand Leagues Under the Sea *by Jules Verne* ∽ THE WAVE ∽ Gulliver's Travels *by Jonathan Swi*
and *by Lewis Carroll* ∽ THE MOUNTAINS ∽ Peter Pan and Wendy *by J.M. Barrie* ∽ THE CAVE ∽ Treasure Island *by Robert Louis Stevenson* and Kidnapped *by Robert Louis Stevenson* ∽ THE FOREST ∽ Little Red Cap *a*
nd Wilhelm Grimm, Snow White and Rose Red *as told by Jacob Grimm and Wilhelm Grimm,* Beauty and the Beast *by Jeanne-Marie Leprince de Beaumont* and Rapunzel *as told by Jacob Grimm and Wilhelm Grimm* ∽ THE MO
winkle, Twinkle, Little Star *by Jane Taylor,* Hush-a-Bye Baby *as adapted by John Newbery* and Brahms' Lullaby *by Johannes Brahms* ∽ THE MOON ∽ Around the Moon *by Jules Verne* ∽ THE WORLD ∽ The Wonderful Wi
Great Expectations *by Charles Dickens,* Adventures of Huckleberry Finn *by Mark Twain,* A Christmas Carol *by Charles Dickens,* Moby Dick *by Herman Melville,* The Secret Garden *by Frances Hodgson Burnett,* Heidi *by Johann*
mily Robinson *by Johann David Wyss,* Robinson Crusoe *by Daniel Defoe,* The Count of Monte Cristo *by Alexandre Dumas,* Kidnapped *by Robert Louis Stevenson,* Gulliver's Travels *by Jonathan Swift* and Twenty Thousand Lea
Under the Sea *by Jules Verne* ∽ THE HOLE ∽ Alice's Adventures in Wonderland *by Lewis Carroll* ∽ THE MOUNTAINS ∽ Peter Pan and Wendy *by J.M. Barrie* ∽ THE CAVE ∽ Treasure Island *by Robert Louis Stevenson a*
umb *as told by Richard Johnson,* The Golden Bird *as told by Jacob Grimm and Wilhelm Grimm,* Snow White and Rose Red *as told by Jacob Grimm and Wilhelm Grimm,* Beauty and the Beast *by Jeanne-Marie Leprince de Beaumon*
elm Grimm ∽ THE CLOUDS ∽ Suo Gân *as adapted by Robert Bryan,* Twinkle, Twinkle, Little Star *by Jane Taylor,* Hush-a-Bye Baby *as adapted by John Newbery* and Brahms' Lullaby *by Johannes Brahms* ∽ THE MOON ∽ A
bbit *by Beatrix Potter,* Alice's Adventures in Wonderland *by Lewis Carroll,* Great Expectations *by Charles Dickens,* Adventures of Huckleberry Finn *by Mark Twain,* A Christmas Carol *by Charles Dickens,* Moby Dick *by Herm*
SEA ∽ The Voyages of Doctor Dolittle *by Hugh Lofting,* The Swiss Family Robinson *by Johann David Wyss,* Robinson Crusoe *by Daniel Defoe,* The Count of Monte Cristo *by Alexandre Dumas,* Kidnapped *by Robert Louis St*
entures of Pinocchio *by Carlo Collodi* and Twenty Thousand Leagues Under the Sea *by Jules Verne* ∽ THE HOLE ∽ Alice's Adventures in Wonderland *by Lewis Carroll* ∽ THE MOUNTAINS ∽ Peter Pan and Wendy *by J.*

n Grimm, Beauty and the Beast by Jeanne-Marie Leprince de Beaumont and Rapunzel as told by Jacob Grimm and Wilhelm Grimm ∽ THE MONSTER ∽ The Legend of Sleepy Hollow by Washington Irving, Frankenstein by M
Newbery and Brahms' Lullaby by Johannes Brahms ∽ THE MOON ∽ Around the Moon by Jules Verne ∽ THE WORLD ∽ The Wonderful Wizard of Oz by L. Frank Baum, The Wind in the Willows by Kenneth Grahame, L
ark Twain, A Christmas Carol by Charles Dickens, Moby Dick by Herman Melville, The Secret Garden by Frances Hodgson Burnett, Heidi by Johanna Spyri, Black Beauty by Anna Sewell, The Legends of King Arthur and His
Count of Monte Cristo by Alexandre Dumas, Kidnapped by Robert Louis Stevenson, Gulliver's Travels by Jonathan Swift and Twenty Thousand Leagues Under the Sea by Jules Verne ∽ THE WAVE ∽ Gulliver's Travels by Jon
Wonderland by Lewis Carroll ∽ THE MOUNTAINS ∽ Peter Pan and Wendy by J.M. Barrie ∽ THE CAVE ∽ Treasure Island by Robert Louis Stevenson and Kidnapped by Robert Louis Stevenson ∽ THE FOREST ∽ Little Re
mm and Wilhelm Grimm, Snow White and Rose Red as told by Jacob Grimm and Wilhelm Grimm, Beauty and the Beast by Jeanne-Marie Leprince de Beaumont and Rapunzel as told by Jacob Grimm and Wilhelm Grimm ∽ THE
ryan, Twinkle, Twinkle, Little Star by Jane Taylor, Hush-a-Bye Baby as adapted by John Newbery and Brahms' Lullaby by Johannes Brahms ∽ THE MOON ∽ Around the Moon by Jules Verne ∽ THE WORLD ∽ The Wonde
arroll, Great Expectations by Charles Dickens, Adventures of Huckleberry Finn by Mark Twain, A Christmas Carol by Charles Dickens, Moby Dick by Herman Melville, The Secret Garden by Frances Hodgson Burnett, Heidi by
wiss Family Robinson by Johann David Wyss, Robinson Crusoe by Daniel Defoe, The Count of Monte Cristo by Alexandre Dumas, Kidnapped by Robert Louis Stevenson, Gulliver's Travels by Jonathan Swift and Twenty Thousa
and Leagues Under the Sea by Jules Verne ∽ THE HOLE ∽ Alice's Adventures in Wonderland by Lewis Carroll ∽ THE MOUNTAINS ∽ Peter Pan and Wendy by J.M. Barrie ∽ THE CAVE ∽ Treasure Island by Robert Lou
Grimm, Tom Thumb as told by Richard Johnson, The Golden Bird as told by Jacob Grimm and Wilhelm Grimm, Snow White and Rose Red as told by Jacob Grimm and Wilhelm Grimm, Beauty and the Beast by Jeanne-Marie Lep
Grimm and Wilhelm Grimm ∽ THE CLOUDS ∽ Suo Gân as adapted by Robert Bryan, Twinkle, Twinkle, Little Star by Jane Taylor, Hush-a-Bye Baby as adapted by John Newbery and Brahms' Lullaby by Johannes Brahms ∽ T
Tale of Peter Rabbit by Beatrix Potter, Alice's Adventures in Wonderland by Lewis Carroll, Great Expectations by Charles Dickens, Adventures of Huckleberry Finn by Mark Twain, A Christmas Carol by Charles Dickens, Mob
Irving ∽ THE SEA ∽ The Voyages of Doctor Dolittle by Hugh Lofting, The Swiss Family Robinson by Johann David Wyss, Robinson Crusoe by Daniel Defoe, The Count of Monte Cristo by Alexandre Dumas, Kidnapped b
David Wyss, The Adventures of Pinocchio by Carlo Collodi and Twenty Thousand Leagues Under the Sea by Jules Verne ∽ THE HOLE ∽ Alice's Adventures in Wonderland by Lewis Carroll ∽ THE MOUNTAINS ∽ Peter
d Wilhelm Grimm, The Golden Goose as told by Jacob Grimm and Wilhelm Grimm, Tom Thumb as told by Richard Johnson, The Golden Bird as told by Jacob Grimm and Wilhelm Grimm, Snow White and Rose Red as told by J
helley and Dracula by Bram Stoker ∽ THE ROPE ∽ Rapunzel as told by Jacob Grimm and Wilhelm Grimm ∽ THE CLOUDS ∽ Suo Gân as adapted by Robert Bryan, Twinkle, Twinkle, Little Star by Jane Taylor, Hush-a-Bye B
men by Louisa May Alcott, The Three Musketeers by Alexandre Dumas, The Tale of Peter Rabbit by Beatrix Potter, Alice's Adventures in Wonderland by Lewis Carroll, Great Expectations by Charles Dickens, Adventures of Hu
Sir Thomas Malory and Sir James Knowles and Rip Van Winkle by Washington Irving ∽ THE SEA ∽ The Voyages of Doctor Dolittle by Hugh Lofting, The Swiss Family Robinson by Johann David Wyss, Robinson Crusoe by D
obinson Crusoe by Daniel Defoe, The Swiss Family Robinson by Johann David Wyss, The Adventures of Pinocchio by Carlo Collodi and Twenty Thousand Leagues Under the Sea by Jules Verne ∽ THE HOLE ∽ Alice's Adve
d by Jacob Grimm and Wilhelm Grimm, Hansel & Gretel as told by Jacob Grimm and Wilhelm Grimm, The Golden Goose as told by Jacob Grimm and Wilhelm Grimm, Tom Thumb as told by Richard Johnson, The Golden Bird a
ER ∽ The Legend of Sleepy Hollow by Washington Irving, Frankenstein by Mary Shelley and Dracula by Bram Stoker ∽ THE ROPE ∽ Rapunzel as told by Jacob Grimm and Wilhelm Grimm ∽ THE CLOUDS ∽ Suo Gân as
of Oz by L. Frank Baum, The Wind in the Willows by Kenneth Grahame, Little Women by Louisa May Alcott, The Three Musketeers by Alexandre Dumas, The Tale of Peter Rabbit by Beatrix Potter, Alice's Adventures in Won
pyri, Black Beauty by Anna Sewell, The Legends of King Arthur and His Knights by Sir Thomas Malory and Sir James Knowles and Rip Van Winkle by Washington Irving ∽ THE SEA ∽ The Voyages of Doctor Dolittle by Hu
s Under the Sea by Jules Verne ∽ THE WAVE ∽ Gulliver's Travels by Jonathan Swift, Robinson Crusoe by Daniel Defoe, The Swiss Family Robinson by Johann David Wyss, The Adventures of Pinocchio by Carlo Collodi and T
Kidnapped by Robert Louis Stevenson ∽ THE FOREST ∽ Little Red Cap as told by Jacob Grimm and Wilhelm Grimm, Hansel & Gretel as told by Jacob Grimm and Wilhelm Grimm, The Golden Goose as told by Jacob Grimm an
d Rapunzel as told by Jacob Grimm and Wilhelm Grimm ∽ THE MONSTER ∽ The Legend of Sleepy Hollow by Washington Irving, Frankenstein by Mary Shelley and Dracula by Bram Stoker ∽ THE ROPE ∽ Rapunzel as to
nd the Moon by Jules Verne ∽ THE WORLD ∽ The Wonderful Wizard of Oz by L. Frank Baum, The Wind in the Willows by Kenneth Grahame, Little Women by Louisa May Alcott, The Three Musketeers by Alexandre Dum
Melville, The Secret Garden by Frances Hodgson Burnett, Heidi by Johanna Spyri, Black Beauty by Anna Sewell, The Legends of King Arthur and His Knights by Sir Thomas Malory and Sir James Knowles and Rip Van Winkle b
son, Gulliver's Travels by Jonathan Swift and Twenty Thousand Leagues Under the Sea by Jules Verne ∽ THE WAVE ∽ Gulliver's Travels by Jonathan Swift, Robinson Crusoe by Daniel Defoe, The Swiss Family Robinson by
Barrie ∽ THE CAVE ∽ Treasure Island by Robert Louis Stevenson and Kidnapped by Robert Louis Stevenson ∽ THE FOREST ∽ Little Red Cap as told by Jacob Grimm and Wilhelm Grimm, Hansel & Gretel as told by Jacob Gri
n Grimm, Beauty and the Beast by Jeanne-Marie Leprince de Beaumont and Rapunzel as told by Jacob Grimm and Wilhelm Grimm ∽ THE MONSTER ∽ The Legend of Sleepy Hollow by Washington Irving, Frankenstein by M
Newbery and Brahms' Lullaby by Johannes Brahms ∽ THE MOON ∽ Around the Moon by Jules Verne ∽ THE WORLD ∽ The Wonderful Wizard of Oz by L. Frank Baum, The Wind in the Willows by Kenneth Grahame, L
ark Twain, A Christmas Carol by Charles Dickens, Moby Dick by Herman Melville, The Secret Garden by Frances Hodgson Burnett, Heidi by Johanna Spyri, Black Beauty by Anna Sewell, The Legends of King Arthur and His
Count of Monte Cristo by Alexandre Dumas, Kidnapped by Robert Louis Stevenson, Gulliver's Travels by Jonathan Swift and Twenty Thousand Leagues Under the Sea by Jules Verne ∽ THE WAVE ∽ Gulliver's Travels by Jon
Wonderland by Lewis Carroll ∽ THE MOUNTAINS ∽ Peter Pan and Wendy by J.M. Barrie ∽ THE CAVE ∽ Treasure Island by Robert Louis Stevenson and Kidnapped by Robert Louis Stevenson ∽ THE FOREST ∽ Little Re
mm and Wilhelm Grimm, Snow White and Rose Red as told by Jacob Grimm and Wilhelm Grimm, Beauty and the Beast by Jeanne-Marie Leprince de Beaumont and Rapunzel as told by Jacob Grimm and Wilhelm Grimm ∽ THE
ryan, Twinkle, Twinkle, Little Star by Jane Taylor, Hush-a-Bye Baby as adapted by John Newbery and Brahms' Lullaby by Johannes Brahms ∽ THE MOON ∽ Around the Moon by Jules Verne ∽ THE WORLD ∽ The Wonder
arroll, Great Expectations by Charles Dickens, Adventures of Huckleberry Finn by Mark Twain, A Christmas Carol by Charles Dickens, Moby Dick by Herman Melville, The Secret Garden by Frances Hodgson Burnett, Heidi by
wiss Family Robinson by Johann David Wyss, Robinson Crusoe by Daniel Defoe, The Count of Monte Cristo by Alexandre Dumas, Kidnapped by Robert Louis Stevenson, Gulliver's Travels by Jonathan Swift and Twenty Thousa
and Leagues Under the Sea by Jules Verne ∽ THE HOLE ∽ Alice's Adventures in Wonderland by Lewis Carroll ∽ THE MOUNTAINS ∽ Peter Pan and Wendy by J.M. Barrie ∽ THE CAVE ∽ Treasure Island by Robert Lou
Grimm, Tom Thumb as told by Richard Johnson, The Golden Bird as told by Jacob Grimm and Wilhelm Grimm, Snow White and Rose Red as told by Jacob Grimm and Wilhelm Grimm, Beauty and the Beast by Jeanne-Marie Lep
Grimm and Wilhelm Grimm ∽ THE CLOUDS ∽ Suo Gân as adapted by Robert Bryan, Twinkle, Twinkle, Little Star by Jane Taylor, Hush-a-Bye Baby as adapted by John Newbery and Brahms' Lullaby by Johannes Brahms ∽ T
Tale of Peter Rabbit by Beatrix Potter, Alice's Adventures in Wonderland by Lewis Carroll, Great Expectations by Charles Dickens, Adventures of Huckleberry Finn by Mark Twain, A Christmas Carol by Charles Dickens, Mob
Irving ∽ THE SEA ∽ The Voyages of Doctor Dolittle by Hugh Lofting, The Swiss Family Robinson by Johann David Wyss, Robinson Crusoe by Daniel Defoe, The Count of Monte Cristo by Alexandre Dumas, Kidnapped b
David Wyss, The Adventures of Pinocchio by Carlo Collodi and Twenty Thousand Leagues Under the Sea by Jules Verne ∽ THE HOLE ∽ Alice's Adventures in Wonderland by Lewis Carroll ∽ THE MOUNTAINS ∽ Peter
d Wilhelm Grimm, The Golden Goose as told by Jacob Grimm and Wilhelm Grimm, Tom Thumb as told by Richard Johnson, The Golden Bird as told by Jacob Grimm and Wilhelm Grimm, Snow White and Rose Red as told by Ja
helley and Dracula by Bram Stoker ∽ THE ROPE ∽ Rapunzel as told by Jacob Grimm and Wilhelm Grimm ∽ THE CLOUDS ∽ Suo Gân as adapted by Robert Bryan, Twinkle, Twinkle, Little Star by Jane Taylor, Hush-a-Bye B
men by Louisa May Alcott, The Three Musketeers by Alexandre Dumas, The Tale of Peter Rabbit by Beatrix Potter, Alice's Adventures in Wonderland by Lewis Carroll, Great Expectations by Charles Dickens, Adventures of Hu
Sir Thomas Malory and Sir James Knowles and Rip Van Winkle by Washington Irving ∽ THE SEA ∽ The Voyages of Doctor Dolittle by Hugh Lofting, The Swiss Family Robinson by Johann David Wyss, Robinson Crusoe by L
obinson Crusoe by Daniel Defoe, The Swiss Family Robinson by Johann David Wyss, The Adventures of Pinocchio by Carlo Collodi and Twenty Thousand Leagues Under the Sea by Jules Verne ∽ THE HOLE ∽ Alice's Adve
d by Jacob Grimm and Wilhelm Grimm, Hansel & Gretel as told by Jacob Grimm and Wilhelm Grimm, The Golden Goose as told by Jacob Grimm and Wilhelm Grimm, Tom Thumb as told by Richard Johnson, The Golden Bird a
ER ∽ The Legend of Sleepy Hollow by Washington Irving, Frankenstein by Mary Shelley and Dracula by Bram Stoker ∽ THE ROPE ∽ Rapunzel as told by Jacob Grimm and Wilhelm Grimm ∽ THE CLOUDS ∽ Suo Gân as
of Oz by L. Frank Baum, The Wind in the Willows by Kenneth Grahame, Little Women by Louisa May Alcott, The Three Musketeers by Alexandre Dumas, The Tale of Peter Rabbit by Beatrix Potter, Alice's Adventures in Won
pyri, Black Beauty by Anna Sewell, The Legends of King Arthur and His Knights by Sir Thomas Malory and Sir James Knowles and Rip Van Winkle by Washington Irving ∽ THE SEA ∽ The Voyages of Doctor Dolittle by Hu
s Under the Sea by Jules Verne ∽ THE WAVE ∽ Gulliver's Travels by Jonathan Swift, Robinson Crusoe by Daniel Defoe, The Swiss Family Robinson by Johann David Wyss, The Adventures of Pinocchio by Carlo Collodi and T
Kidnapped by Robert Louis Stevenson ∽ THE FOREST ∽ Little Red Cap as told by Jacob Grimm and Wilhelm Grimm, Hansel & Gretel as told by Jacob Grimm and Wilhelm Grimm, The Golden Goose as told by Jacob Grimm an
d Rapunzel as told by Jacob Grimm and Wilhelm Grimm ∽ THE MONSTER ∽ The Legend of Sleepy Hollow by Washington Irving, Frankenstein by Mary Shelley and Dracula by Bram Stoker ∽ THE ROPE ∽ Rapunzel as to
nd the Moon by Jules Verne ∽ THE WORLD ∽ The Wonderful Wizard of Oz by L. Frank Baum, The Wind in the Willows by Kenneth Grahame, Little Women by Louisa May Alcott, The Three Musketeers by Alexandre Dum
Melville, The Secret Garden by Frances Hodgson Burnett, Heidi by Johanna Spyri, Black Beauty by Anna Sewell, The Legends of King Arthur and His Knights by Sir Thomas Malory and Sir James Knowles and Rip Van Winkle b
son, Gulliver's Travels by Jonathan Swift and Twenty Thousand Leagues Under the Sea by Jules Verne ∽ THE WAVE ∽ Gulliver's Travels by Jonathan Swift, Robinson Crusoe by Daniel Defoe, The Swiss Family Robinson by
Barrie ∽ THE CAVE ∽ Treasure Island by Robert Louis Stevenson and Kidnapped by Robert Louis Stevenson ∽ THE FOREST ∽ Little Red Cap as told by Jacob Grimm and Wilhelm Grimm, Hansel & Gretel as told by Jacob Gri

First published 2016 by Walker Books Ltd
87 Vauxhall Walk, London SE11 5HJ

This edition published 2019

2 4 6 8 10 9 7 5 3 1

This book was hand-lettered and the typographical landscapes
were typeset in Adobe Garamond Pro.

Printed in China

British Library Cataloguing in Publication Data:
a catalogue record for this book is available from the British Library

ISBN 978-1-4063-8604-2

www.walker.co.uk

WALKER BOOKS
AND SUBSIDIARIES

LONDON • BOSTON • SYDNEY • AUCKLAND

A Child of Books

OLIVER JEFFERS
SAM WINSTON

For Lila, from Sam
For Luella, from Oliver

"The universe is made of stories, not of atoms."
Muriel Rukeyser, "The Speed of Darkness", 1968

And for Hurbinek

"Hurbinek died in the first days of March 1945, free but not redeemed.
Nothing remains of him: he bears witness through these words of mine."
Primo Levi, *If This Is a Man / The Truce*, 1947

I am a
child of Books.

I come From a WORLD of STORIES

and upon my
IMAGINATION

The Voyages of Doctor Dolittle It was all so new and different: just the sky above ship, which was to be our house and our street, our home and our garden, for so many days t so tiny in all this wide water – so tiny and yet so snug, sufficient, safe. I looked around me an a deep breath. The Doctor was at the wheel steering the boat which was now leaping and plu through the waves. (I had expected to feel seasick at first but was delighted to find that I didn't.) had been told off to go downstairs and prepare dinner for us. Chee-Chee was coiling up ropes in the and laying them in neat piles. My work was fastening down the things on the deck so that nothing about if the weather should grow rough when we got further from the land. Jip was up in the peak boat with ears cocked and nose stuck out – like a statue, so still – his keen old eyes keeping a sharp look- floating wrecks, sand-bars, and other dangers. Each one of us had some special job to do, part of the pro ning of a ship. Even old Polynesia was taking the sea's temperature with the Doctor's bath-thermome on the end of a string, to make sure there were no icebergs near us. As I listened to her swearing to herself because she couldn't read the pesky figures in the fading light, I realized that the voyage begun in earnest and that very soon it would be night – my first night at sea! **Robinson Crusoe** rowed, or rather driven about a league and a half, as we reckoned it, a raging wave, mountain came rolling astern of us, and plainly bade us expect the coup de grace. It took us with such vo that it overset the boat at once; and separating us as well from the boat as from one another, g a no time to say, "O God!" for we were all swallowed up in a moment. Nothing can describe th m usion of thought which I felt, when I sunk into the water; for though I swam very well, yet I c wt not deliver myself from the waves so as to draw breath, till that wave having driven me, or ra Pa arried me, a vast way towards the shore, and having spent itself, went back, and left me upon on almost dry, but half dead with the water I took in. I had such presence of mind, as well as blu seeing myself nearer the mainland than I expected, I got upon my feet, and endeavour ne but I soon found it was impossible to avoid it; for I saw the sea come after me as high as a grs the and as furious as an enemy, which I had no means or strength to contend with: my business so held my breath, and raise myself upon the water if I could; and so, by swimming, to preservera thing, and pilot myself towards the shore, if possible, my greatest concern now being that the s when it gave me a great way towards the sea. **The Swiss Family Robinson** Amid the roar of the th es I suddenly heard the cry of "Land! land!", while at the same instant the ship struck wi while at the same instant the ship struck and seemed to threaten her immediate htful shock, which threw everyone to the deck, and seemed to threaten her immediate uction. Dreadful sounds betokened the breaking up of the ship, and the roaring water in on all sides. Then the voice of the captain was heard above the tumult, shoutin away the boats! We are lost!" "Lost!" I exclaimed, and the word went like a dag ny heart; but seeing my children's terror renewed, I composed myself, calling out "Take courage, my boys! We are all above water yet. There is the land not far, us do our best to reach it. You know God helps those that help themselves!" W left them and went on deck. What was my horror when through the foam a ay I beheld the only remaining boat leave the ship, the last of the seamen sprin er and push off, regardless of my cries and entreaties that we might be allowed chance of preserving their lives. My voice was drowned in the howling of the bl even had the crew wished it, the return of the boat was impossible. Casting despairingly around, I became gradually aware that our position was by no m peless, inasmuch as the stern of the ship containing our cabin was jammed be two high rocks, and was partly raised from among the breakers which dashed ore part to pieces. As the clouds of mist and rain drove past, I could make out, gh rents in the vaporous curtain, a line of rocky coast, and, rugged as it was, art bounded towards it as a sign of help in the hour of need. Yet the sense of ney and forsaken condition weighed heavily upon me as I returned to my fa constraining myself to say with a smile, "Courage, dear ones! Although our go will never sail more, she is so placed that our cabin will remain above water, omorrow, if the wind and waves abate, I see no reason why we should not get a **The Count of Monte Cristo** He saw overhead a black and tempestuous sky, ac the wind was driving clouds that occasionally suffered a twinkling star to appe fore him was the vast expanse of waters, sombre and terrible, whose waves foame roared as if before the approach of a storm. Behind him, blacker than the sea, bla an the sky, rose phantom-like the vast stone structure, whose projecting crags see like arms extended to seize their prey, and on the highest rock was a torch lighting t ures. He fancied that these two forms were looking at the sea; doubtless these stran diggers had heard his cry. Dantès dived again, and remained a long time beneath th Th s was an easy feat to him, for he usually attracted a crowd of spectators in the bay voyages, when at Marseilles when he swam there, and was unanimously declared to be t swimmer in the port. When he came up again the light had disappeared. Sometimes, the lighthouse at Marseilles when he swam there, and I have seen the heavens

I Float.

Captain Hook
Dr. Dolittle

Robinson Crusoe
Gulliver's Travels
Pinocchio
Sinbad

its wings. Then I felt that my vessel was a vain refuge, that trembled and shook before the... The tempest was let loose and beating the atmosphere with its mighty wings; from time to time... flash of lightning stretched across the heavens like a fiery serpent, lighting up the clouds that... on in vast chaotic waves. The thieves looked at one another with low murmurs, and a stor... ...ered over the head of the aristocratic prisoner, raised less by his own words than by the... of the keeper. The latter, sure of quelling the tempest when the waves became too viole... ...wed them to rise to a certain pitch that he might be revenged on the importunate An... ...d besides it would afford him some recreation during the day. **Kidnapped** While I... ...ling the brig, I spied a tract of water lying between us where no great waves came, b... ...ch yet boiled white all over and bristled in the moon with rings and bubbles. Some... ...he whole tract swung to one side, like the tail of a live serpent; sometimes, for a gl... ...it would all disappear and then boil up again. What it was I had no guess, which... ...time increased my fear of it; but I now know it must have been the roost or tid... ...which had carried me away so fast and tumbled me about so cruelly, and at last,... ...ed of that play, had flung out me and the spare yard upon its landward margin. ...*. **Gulliver's Travels** It would not be proper, for some reasons, to trouble the re... ...iculars of our adventures in those seas; let it suffice to inform him, that in our p... ...hence to the East Indies, we were driven by a violent storm to the north-west... Diemen's Land. By an observation, we found ourselves in the latitude of 30 d... 2 minutes south. Twelve of our crew were dead by immoderate labour and il... the rest were in a very weak condition. On the 5th of November, which was th... ...nning of summer in those parts, the weather being very hazy, the seamen spied... ...within half a cable's length of the ship; but the wind was so strong, that we we... ...en directly upon it, and immediately split. Six of the crew, of whom I was one... ...let down the boat into the sea, made a shift to get clear of the ship and the r... ...We rowed, by my computation, about three leagues, till we were able to work n... ...ger, being already spent with labour while we were in the ship. We therefore tru... ...ourselves to the mercy of the waves, and in about half an hour the boat was over... ...a sudden flurry from the north. What became of my companions in the boat, a... ...as of those who escaped on the rock, or were left in the vessel, I cannot tell; but c... ...de they were all lost. For my own part, I swam as fortune directed me, and was p... ...I forward by wind and tide. I often let my legs drop, and could feel no bottom; but... I was almost gone, and able to struggle no longer, I found myself within my de... ...nd by this time the storm was much abated. The declivity was so small, that I wo... ...near a mile before I got to the shore, which I conjectured was about eight o'c... ...in the evening. I then advanced forward near half a mile, but could not disc... ...y sign of houses or inhabitants; at least I was in so weak a condition, that... ...not observe them. I was extremely tired, and with that, and the heat of... ...eather, and about half a pint of brandy that I drank as I left the ship,... ...d myself much inclined to sleep. I lay down on the grass, which was v... ...hor and soft, where I slept sounder than ever I remember to have d... ...n my life, and, as I reckoned, about nine hours; for when I awaked,... ...just day-light. I attempted to rise, but was not able to stir: for, as I... ...ned to lie on my back, I found my arms and legs were strongly fa... ...on each side to the ground; and my hair, which was long and... ...tied down in the same manner. I likewise felt several slende... ...across my body, from my arm-pits to my thighs. I could only lo... ...wards; the sun began to grow hot, and the light offended my e... ...heard a confused noise about me; but in the posture I lay,... ...ee nothing except the sky. In a little time I felt something al... ...ing on my left leg, which advancing gently forward over my... ...came almost up to my chin; when, bending my eyes down... ...nches high, with a bow and arrow in his hands, and a quive... back. In the mean time, I felt at least forty more. I was of... ...utmost astonishment, and roared so loud, that they all ran... ...n a fright; and some of them, as I was afterwards told, wer... ...with the falls they got by leaping from my sides upon the g... ...l. However, they soon returned, and one of them, who ven... ...so far as to get a full sight of my face, lifting up his hands a... ...s by way of admiration, cried out in a shrill but distinct voi... *...inah degul:* the others repeated the same words several times,... ...hen I knew not what they meant. I lay all this while, as the re... ...may believe, in great uneasiness. **Twenty Thousand Leagues** **Under the Sea.** So our salvation lay totally in the hands of... ...sterious helmsmen steering this submersible, and if it mace a...

of in south... summer which was i ... those parts, beginning to ... being very hazy, the weather ... the seamen spied a rock within ... not be proper; for some reasons, ... half a cable's length of the ship; ... but the wind was so strong, that ... were driven directly upon it, and ... e crew, of whom I was one, having le ... t down the boat into the sea, made a s ... hift to get clear of the ship and the rock. **Gulliver's Travels** Six of t ... e rowed, by my computation, about three ... ues, till we were able to work no longer, bei ... ng already spent with labour while we were i ... the ship. We therefore trusted ourselves to the ... overset by a sudden flurry from the north. What be ... of my companions in the boat, as well as of those who ... caped on the rock, or were left in the vessel, I cannot tell: b ... ut conclude they were all lost. For my own part, I swam as f ... une directed me, pushed forward by wind and tide. I often let ... my legs drop, and felt no bottom; but when I was almost gone, ... able to struggle no longer, I found myself within my depth; and ... me the storm was much abated. **The Swiss Family Robinson** For many days ... we had been tempest-tossed. Six times had the darkness closed over a wild an ... conjecture could be formed as to our whereabouts. The crew had lost heart, and were utterly exhausted by incessant labour. The riven masts had gone by the board, leaks had been sprung in every direction, and the water, which rushed in, gained upon us rapidly. Instead of reckless oaths, the seamen now uttered frantic cries to God for mercy, mingled with strange and of ... terrific scene, and returning light as often brought but renewed distress, for the raging storm increased in fury until on the seventh day all hope was lost. We were driven completely out of ... ous vows, to be performed should deliverance be granted. Every man on board alternately commended his soul to his Creator, and strove to bethink himself of some means of savi ... every direction, and the water is very rough and ... raging wave, mountain-like, came rolling astern of us, and plainly bade us expect, at once; and separating us as well from the boat he coup de grace. It took us with such fury, that it overset the boat for we were all swallowed up in a mo

driven, about a lea and a half, as we reckon

rowed, or rath

A we ha

of our situation seemed less overwhelming. "Ah," thought I, "the Lord will hear our prayer! He will help us." Our hearts were overpowered by terror. "Dear children," said I, "if the Lord will, He can save us ... and deliverance for his dear parents and brothers, as though quite forgetting himself, one after another praying with deep earnestness and emotion. Fritz, in particular, appeared closely ... and then gave a sharp cry: "It's my father!" Meanwhile, the little boat, tossed about by the angry waters, appeared and disappeared ... **The Adventures of Pinocchio** "Where is the little boat?" "There. Straight ahead," ... asked Pinocchio of a little old woman, pointing to a tiny shadow, no bigger than a nutshell, floating on the sea. Pinocchio looked closely. After looking closely ... , "I looked round upon my family in the midst of these horrors. We knelt down together, ... wered the little old woman, ... and swam like a fish in the rough water. Now and again he disappeared ... ves. And Pinocchio, standing on a high rock, tired out with searching, waved to him with hand and cap and even ... ank as I looked round upon my weeping wife looked bravely up, and, as the boys clustered round her, she began to cheer and encourage them with calm and loving words. I rejoiced to see ...

ards my weeping wife looked bravely up ...
arful peril: if not, let us calmly yield our lives into His hand, ...
er was ready to break as I gazed on my dear ones. ...
" looked as if Geppetto, though far away from the shore, recognized his son, for he seemed to be trying to r ...
derstand that he would come back if he were able, but the sea was so heavy that he could do nothing ...
uddenly a huge wave came and the boat disappeared. They waited and waited for it, but it was ...
" said the fisher folk on the shore, whispering a prayer as they turned to go home. Just the ...
was heard. Turning around, the fisher folk saw Pinocchio dive into the sea and hea ...
"I'll save him! I'll save my father!" The Marionette, being made of wood, floa ...
ear once more. In a twinkling, he was far away from land. At last ...
rely lost to view. "Poor boy!" cried the fisher folk on the sh ...
they mumbled a few prayers, as they returned home. We could ...
d Leagues Under the Sea Near four o'clock i ...
submersible picked up speed. ...
h this dizzying rush, and the wave ...
cross a big mooring ri ...
close range. Fortunately Ne ...
the topside of thi ...
and w ...
d de ...

I have SAILED
Across a SEA
of WORDS

To ask if you will
come AWAY with me.

SOME PEOPLE have
FORGOTTEN where
I live

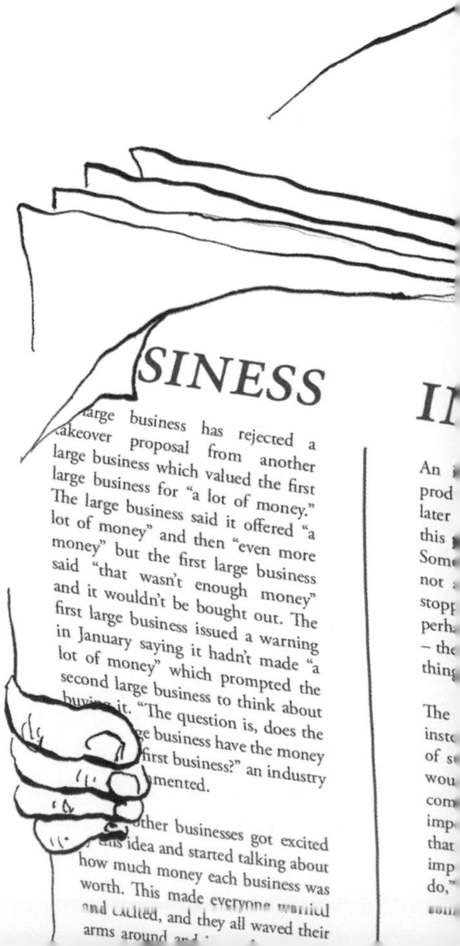

SINESS   II

large business has rejected a
takeover proposal from another
large business which valued the first
large business for "a lot of money."
The large business said it offered "a
lot of money" and then "even more
money" but the first large business
said "that wasn't enough money"
and it wouldn't be bought out. The
first large business issued a warning
in January saying it hadn't made "a
lot of money" which prompted the
second large business to think about
buying it. "The question is, does the
large business have the money
first business?" an industry
commented.

other businesses got excited
this idea and started talking about
how much money each business was
worth. This made everyone worried
and excited, and they all waved their
arms around

An
prod
later
this
Some
not
stopp
perha
– the
thing

The
inste
of s
wou
com
imp
that
imp
do,

IMPORTANT THINGS

ortant company is to stop
g some important stuff by
year. It said no one wanted
cular bit of important stuff.
 from a website said – "It's
ll surprising that they have
 producing this thing –
it's not so important after all
ain issue now is to find other
at might be important."

npany announced it would
ocus on producing other bits
that they hoped the public
ind important. "We remain
red to providing people with
nt things and if we can't do
en we will pretend they are
nt and hopefully that will
d the leading inventor at the
y.

also said they would stop making this
particular bit of stuff as they also thought
it might not be as important as they once
thought it was. "What makes something
really important nowadays is how much
money we spend on it and if we spend
vast amounts of money on it, then that
obviously means it's going to be really
important and we will certainly make a
hoo-haa about it when we put it in the
shops," said the Big Boss.

One customer did respond to this
comment with "My cat is very important
and that didn't cost anything!" to which
the important company wrote a letter
in response that said, "Dear Customer,
we understand that you think your cat
is very important but unfortunately you
are wrong in this matter. Our leading
inventor says he d

Serious Stuff

A group of serious people passed on concerns about a serious document that has been lost by a serious
organization. The serious people asked officials it had looked at this serious document last y
document – the serious organization initially said it had looked at this serious document last y
concluded that "it wasn't that serious" and then went on to say "we have lost it." Someone els
looked at this document said "actually it was serious and I hope they find it." In an earlier ver
story, we reported that the serious
organization had started looking
for the serious document. In fact,
they started looking last year.
So far they have looked "under
chairs, rugs, and even down a
sofa." Someone suggested to try
looking "on the computer," but
that was unsuccessful as it wasn't
turned on.

In other cases like this – when
someone says "this is serious" and
the other says "no it isn't – they
often have to find a third person
to tell them whether it's serious

THE FACTS

Scientists have discovered a
new fact. In one test, nearly
half the subjects proved the
fact, it was revealed. The
findings, which came from
first watching people and
then quizzing them, have
attracted criticism from some
other scientists.

The paper, published in a
magazine about facts, said
that their fact was true.
A professor, who led the
research at a university, said:
study demonstrated

kind of thing but for
who don't – it could be rather
alarming.

In fact, other researchers in
the field have said the findings
are overstated. The authors
say this 'fact' might have
been overlooked in research.
Their work began with several
trials involving people who
were shut in a small room
and tested. After 6, 12, or 15
minutes, they were asked if
they had discovered this fact.
On average, their answers
were near the middle of a
int scale.

"It
is
a long
tail, certainly,"
said Alice,
looking down
with wonder at
the Mouse's tail;
"but why do you
call it sad?" And
she kept puzzling
about it while the
Mouse was speaking,
so that her idea of the
tale was something like
this: "Fury said to a mouse,
That he met in the house, 'Let
us both go to law: I will prosecute
YOU.—Come, I'll take no
denial; We must have a trial:
For really this morning I've
nothing to do.' Said the mouse
to the cur, 'Such a trial, dear sir,
With no jury or judge, would
be wasting our breath.' 'I'll be
judge, I'll be jury,' said cunning
old Fury: 'I'll try the whole cause, and
condemn you to death.' *Alice's Adventures
in Wonderland* The rabbit-hole went strai
then dipped suddenly down, so su   that Alice had not a
moment to think about sto   lf before she found herself falling down what seemed to be a very deep well.
Either the well was very deep, or she fell very slowly, for she had plenty of time as she went down to look about her, and to

nothing of tumbling down stairs! How brave they'll all think me at home! W

Down, down, down. Would the fall never come to an

getting somewhere near the centre

Presently she began a

But along these WORDS
I can show you the WAY.

onder what was going to happen next. First, she tried to look down and make out what   but it was too dark

y, I wouldn't say anything about it, even if I fell off the top of the   was very likely true.

end? "I wonder how many miles I've fallen by this time   aloud. "I must

f the earth. Let me see: that would be four thousand   miles down, I

ain. "I wonder if I shall fall right through the earth   How funny

Down, down, down. There was nothing else to do   so Alice soon

WE will TRAVEL over
MOUNTAINS of MAKE-BElieve

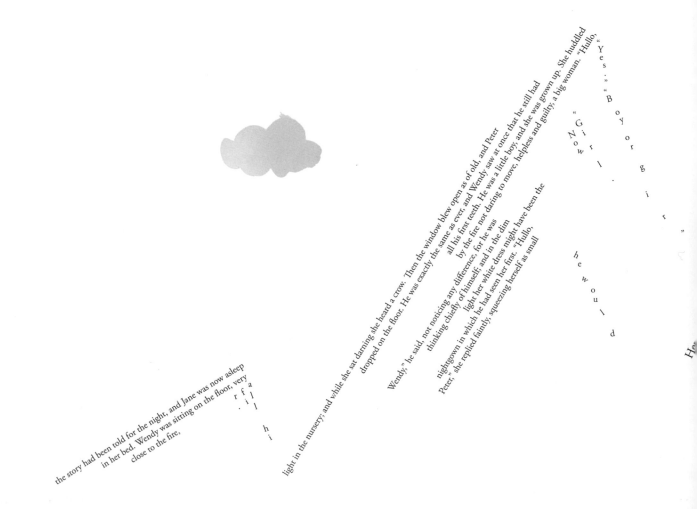

the story had been told for the night, and Jane was now asleep in her bed. Wendy was sitting on the floor, very close to the fire, so as to see to darn, for there was no other light in the nursery; and while she sat darning she heard a crow. Then the window blew open as of old, and Peter dropped on the floor. He was exactly the same as ever, and Wendy saw at once that he still had all his first teeth. He was a little boy, and she was grown up. She huddled by the fire not daring to move, helpless and guilty, a big woman.

"Hullo, Wendy," he said, not noticing any difference, for he was thinking chiefly of himself; and in the dim light her white dress might have been the nightgown in which he had seen her first. "Hullo, Peter," she replied faintly, squeezing herself as small as she could. Something inside her was crying "Woman, woman, let go of me."

"Hullo, where is John?" he asked, suddenly missing the third bed.

"John is not here now," she gasped.

"Is Michael asleep?" he asked, with a careless glance at Jane.

"Yes," she answered; and now she felt that she was untrue to Jane as well as to Peter.

"That is not Michael," she said quickly, lest a judgment should fall on her.

Peter looked. "Hullo, is it a new one?"

"Yes."

"Boy or girl?"

"Girl."

Now surely he would understand; but not a bit of it.

"Peter," she said, faltering, "are you expecting me to fly away with you?"

"Of course; that is why I have come." He added a little sternly, "Have you forgotten that this is spring-cleaning time?"

She knew it was useless to say that he had let many spring-cleaning times pass.

"I can't come," she said apologetically, "I have forgotten how to fly."

"I'll soon teach you again."

"O Peter, don't waste the fairy dust on me."

She had risen; and now at last a fear assailed him. "What is it?" he cried, shrinking.

"I will turn up the light," she said, "and then you can see for yourself."

For almost the only time in his life that I know of, Peter was afraid. "Don't turn up the light," he cried.

She let her hands play in the hair of the tragic boy. She was not a little girl heart-broken about him; she was a grown woman smiling at it all, but they were wet smiles.

Then she turned up the light, and Peter saw. He gave a cry of pain; and when the tall beautiful creature stooped to lift him in her arms he drew back sharply.

"What is it?" he cried again.

She had to tell him.

"I am old, Peter. I am ever so much more than twenty. I grew up long ago."

"You promised not to!"

"I couldn't help it. I am a married woman, Peter."

"No, you're not."

"Yes, and the little girl in the bed is my baby."

"No, she's not."

Peter Pan and Wendy

...would scarcely carry her now. on his shoulder and gave his nose a loving bite. She whispered to her chamber; lay down on the bed. His head almost filled the fourth wall of her little room as he knelt near her in distress. Every moment her light was growing fainter; and he knew that if it went out she would be no more. She liked his tears so much that she put out her beautiful finger and let them run over it. Her voice was so low that at first he could not make out what she said. Then he made it out. She was saying that she thought she could get well again if children believed in fairies. Peter flung out his arms. There were no children there; and it was night-time; but he addressed all who might be dreaming of the Neverland, and who were therefore nearer to him than you think: boys and girls in their nighties. "Do you believe?" he cried. Tink sat up in bed almost briskly to listen to her fate. She fancied she heard answers in the affirmative, and then again she wasn't sure. "What do you think?" she asked Peter. "If you believe," he shouted to them, "clap your hands; don't let Tink die." Many clapped. Some didn't. A few beasts hissed. The clapping stopped suddenly; as if countless mothers had rushed to their nurseries to see what on earth was happening; but already Tink was saved. First her voice grew strong, then she popped out of bed, then she was flashing through the room more merry and impudent than ever. She never thought of thanking those who believed, but she would have liked to get at the ones who had hissed. "And now to rescue Wendy!"

The moon was riding in a cloudy heaven, wearing weapons on else, little, you stupe t, his Perilous tree,

It had hoped to fly It was not such He had chosen.

...son, and she ran out of the room to try to think. Peter continued to cry, and soon his sobs woke Jane. She sat up in bed, and was interested at once. "Boy," she said, "why are you crying?" Peter rose and bowed to her, and she bowed to him from the bed. "Hullo," he said. "Hullo," said Jane. "My name is Peter Pan," he explained. "Yes, I know." "I came back for my mother," he told her, "to take her to the Neverland." "Yes, I know," Jane said, "I have been waiting for Peter Pan, be told her sitting on the bed."

DISCOVER TREASURE in the DARKNESS.

dancing to and fro through
beautiful flowers
Little Red Cap was takin
happy Little Red Cap

Little **Red Cap** It was a

Once upon a time there dwelt near a large wood

Hansel & Gretel

"What will become of us? children, now that we feed our How can poor

woodcutter, two children discovered in his hollow under the roots a goose with his wife and plumage of pure gold

a little boy called Hansel and named Gretel, a girl

The Golden Goose Dummerly set to the work, and cut down the when it fell tree

"Oh Father, cried shall be in the cart

Tom Thumb

One day, as she was getting into

Little Red Cap

Then the fox said, "Do not
you good counsel
shoot
the golden bird.
put
want to bird.

They saw a beautiful child
sight passed from her eyes
opened her eyes
into the wood
in a snow white
The Golden Bird
She arose white

Snow White & Rose Red It all
word but said no
Once, when they had spent the night in the wood and the
the wood bright sunrise awoke them
Beauty & The Beast

thus standing
he was
large forest
a tree
Rapunzel, Rapunzel,
Let down your hair.

9...
8
7
6

WE can lose
ourselves in FORESTS
of FAIRY Tales

and ESCAPE MONSTERS in HAUNTED CASTLES.

she had magnificent long hair, fine as spun gold, and when she heard the voice of the witch, she unfastened the braided tresses, wound them round one of the hooks of the window above, and then the hair fell down

we will sleep

in clouds of song

different directions, having an opportunity of gazing at the firmament through the Moon through the lower and the upper lights of the Projectile. Ardan and the Captain had co... to operating on the bottom light. **Around the Moon** But Barbican was the first to get th... ...ng: "No, my friends!" he exclaimed, in tones of derided emo... ...h; nor are we lying in the botto...

and sHOUT as
LOUD as
we like
in SPACE.

For THIS is OUR WORld

a kiss!

d'Artagnan

Mr

"wake up, Alice dear!" said her sister.

morning as a
behind bird unusual went on
three
friends would take a stroll together in the Wild Wood.
wondrous

awake
dream
come from?" "From the Land of Oz," said Dorothy

When Mrs. Medlock looked she threw up her

of motherly love, gratitude, and humility,

gave a little
And so, as Tiny

moist with gratitude though beaming with joy

the evening mists were rising now

observed, God bless Us, Every One

to the more

Aunt Sally

and sivilize me, and I can't

here
is Toto

look!

There goes the great Mr Toad!

OUR HOUSE is a Home of

INVENTIon

I am a child of books. I come from a world of stories

our   world   we've   made   from   stories   our   house   is   a

where ANYONE at ALL can come

home   of   invention   where   anyone   at   all   can   come

For IMAGINATION is FREE

The Golden Goose *as told by* Jacob Grimm and Wilhelm Grimm, **Tom Thumb** *as told by Richard Johnson*, **The Golden Bird** *as told by Jacob Grimm and Wilhelm Grimm*, **Snow White and Rose Red** *as told by Jacob Grimm and Wil-*
Bram Stoker ✧ THE ROPE ✧ **Rapunzel** *as told by Jacob Grimm and Wilhelm Grimm* ✧ THE CLOUDS ✧ **Suo Gân** *as adapted by Robert Bryan*, **Twinkle, Twinkle, Little Star** *by Jane Taylor*, **Hush-a-Bye Baby** *as adapted by*
Alcott, **The Three Musketeers** *by Alexandre Dumas*, **The Tale of Peter Rabbit** *by Beatrix Potter*, **Alice's Adventures in Wonderland** *by Lewis Carroll*, **Great Expectations** *by Charles Dickens*, **Adventures of Huckleberry Finn** *by*
alory and Sir James Knowles and **Rip Van Winkle** *by Washington Irving* ✧ THE SEA ✧ **The Voyages of Doctor Dolittle** *by Hugh Lofting*, **The Swiss Family Robinson** *by Johann David Wyss*, **Robinson Crusoe** *by Daniel Defoe,*
Crusoe by Daniel Defoe, **The Swiss Family Robinson** *by Johann David Wyss*, **The Adventures of Pinocchio** *by Carlo Collodi* and **Twenty Thousand Leagues Under the Sea** *by Jules Verne* ✧ THE HOLE ✧ **Alice's Adventures**
nm and Wilhelm Grimm, **Hansel & Gretel** *as told by Jacob Grimm and Wilhelm Grimm*, **The Golden Goose** *as told by Jacob Grimm and Wilhelm Grimm*, **Tom Thumb** *as told by Richard Johnson*, **The Golden Bird** *as told by Jacob*
nd of Sleepy Hollow by Washington Irving, **Frankenstein** *by Mary Shelley* and **Dracula** *by Bram Stoker* ✧ THE ROPE ✧ **Rapunzel** *as told by Jacob Grimm and Wilhelm Grimm* ✧ THE CLOUDS ✧ **Suo Gân** *as adapted by Rober*
k Baum, **The Wind in the Willows** *by Kenneth Grahame*, **Little Women** *by Louisa May Alcott*, **The Three Musketeers** *by Alexandre Dumas*, **The Tale of Peter Rabbit** *by Beatrix Potter*, **Alice's Adventures in Wonderland** *by Lewis*
auty by Anna Sewell, **The Legends of King Arthur and His Knights** *by Sir Thomas Malory and Sir James Knowles and* **Rip Van Winkle** *by Washington Irving* ✧ THE SEA ✧ **The Voyages of Doctor Dolittle** *by Hugh Lofting*, **The**
Sea by Jules Verne ✧ THE WAVE ✧ **Gulliver's Travels** *by Jonathan Swift*, **Robinson Crusoe** *by Daniel Defoe*, **The Swiss Family Robinson** *by Johann David Wyss*, **The Adventures of Pinocchio** *by Carlo Collodi* and **Twenty Tho**
ed by Robert Louis Stevenson ✧ THE FOREST ✧ **Little Red Cap** *as told by Jacob Grimm and Wilhelm Grimm*, **Hansel & Gretel** *as told by Jacob Grimm and Wilhelm Grimm*, **The Golden Goose** *as told by Jacob Grimm and Wilhel*
nzel as told by Jacob Grimm and Wilhelm Grimm ✧ THE MONSTER ✧ **The Legend of Sleepy Hollow** *by Washington Irving*, **Frankenstein** *by Mary Shelley* and **Dracula** *by Bram Stoker* ✧ THE ROPE ✧ **Rapunzel** *as told by*
he Moon by Jules Verne ✧ THE WORLD ✧ **The Wonderful Wizard of Oz** *by L. Frank Baum*, **The Wind in the Willows** *by Kenneth Grahame*, **Little Women** *by Louisa May Alcott*, **The Three Musketeers** *by Alexandre Dumas,*
he Secret Garden by Frances Hodgson Burnett, **Heidi** *by Johanna Spyri*, **Black Beauty** *by Anna Sewell*, **The Legends of King Arthur and His Knights** *by Sir Thomas Malory and Sir James Knowles and* **Rip Van Winkle** *by Washing*
Gulliver's Travels *by Jonathan Swift* and **Twenty Thousand Leagues Under the Sea** *by Jules Verne* ✧ THE WAVE ✧ **Gulliver's Travels** *by Jonathan Swift*, **Robinson Crusoe** *by Daniel Defoe*, **The Swiss Family Robinson** *by Joha*
✧ THE CAVE ✧ **Treasure Island** *by Robert Louis Stevenson* and **Kidnapped** *by Robert Louis Stevenson* ✧ THE FOREST ✧ **Little Red Cap** *as told by Jacob Grimm and Wilhelm Grimm*, **Hansel & Gretel** *as told by Jacob Grimm*
Grimm, **Beauty and the Beast** *by Jeanne-Marie Leprince de Beaumont* and **Rapunzel** *as told by Jacob Grimm and Wilhelm Grimm* ✧ THE MONSTER ✧ **The Legend of Sleepy Hollow** *by Washington Irving*, **Frankenstein** *by Mar*
ery and **Brahms' Lullaby** *by Johannes Brahms* ✧ THE MOON ✧ **Around the Moon** *by Jules Verne* ✧ THE WORLD ✧ **The Wonderful Wizard of Oz** *by L. Frank Baum*, **The Wind in the Willows** *by Kenneth Grahame*, **Little**
in, **A Christmas Carol** *by Charles Dickens*, **Moby Dick** *by Herman Melville*, **The Secret Garden** *by Frances Hodgson Burnett*, **Heidi** *by Johanna Spyri*, **Black Beauty** *by Anna Sewell*, **The Legends of King Arthur and His Knights**
Monte Cristo by Alexandre Dumas, **Kidnapped** *by Robert Louis Stevenson*, **Gulliver's Travels** *by Jonathan Swift* and **Twenty Thousand Leagues Under the Sea** *by Jules Verne* ✧ THE WAVE ✧ **Gulliver's Travels** *by Jonathan Swif*
nd Lewis Carroll ✧ THE MOUNTAINS ✧ **Peter Pan and Wendy** *by J.M. Barrie* ✧ THE CAVE ✧ **Treasure Island** *by Robert Louis Stevenson* and **Kidnapped** *by Robert Louis Stevenson* ✧ THE FOREST ✧ **Little Red Cap** *as*
d Wilhelm Grimm, **Snow White and Rose Red** *as told by Jacob Grimm and Wilhelm Grimm*, **Beauty and the Beast** *by Jeanne-Marie Leprince de Beaumont* and **Rapunzel** *as told by Jacob Grimm and Wilhelm Grimm* ✧ THE MON*
inkle, Twinkle, Little Star by Jane Taylor, **Hush-a-Bye Baby** *as adapted by John Newbery* and **Brahms' Lullaby** *by Johannes Brahms* ✧ THE MOON ✧ **Around the Moon** *by Jules Verne* ✧ THE WORLD ✧ **The Wonderful Wiz**
reat Expectations by Charles Dickens, **Adventures of Huckleberry Finn** *by Mark Twain*, **A Christmas Carol** *by Charles Dickens*, **Moby Dick** *by Herman Melville*, **The Secret Garden** *by Frances Hodgson Burnett*, **Heidi** *by Johann*
ily Robinson by Johann David Wyss, **Robinson Crusoe** *by Daniel Defoe*, **The Count of Monte Cristo** *by Alexandre Dumas*, **Kidnapped** *by Robert Louis Stevenson*, **Gulliver's Travels** *by Jonathan Swift* and **Twenty Thousand Leag**
Under the Sea by Jules Verne ✧ THE HOLE ✧ **Alice's Adventures in Wonderland** *by Lewis Carroll* ✧ THE MOUNTAINS ✧ **Peter Pan and Wendy** *by J.M. Barrie* ✧ THE CAVE ✧ **Treasure Island** *by Robert Louis Stevenson an*
mb as told by Richard Johnson, **The Golden Bird** *as told by Jacob Grimm and Wilhelm Grimm*, **Snow White and Rose Red** *as told by Jacob Grimm and Wilhelm Grimm*, **Beauty and the Beast** *by Jeanne-Marie Leprince de Beaumon*
lm Grimm ✧ THE CLOUDS ✧ **Suo Gân** *as adapted by Robert Bryan*, **Twinkle, Twinkle, Little Star** *by Jane Taylor*, **Hush-a-Bye Baby** *as adapted by John Newbery* and **Brahms' Lullaby** *by Johannes Brahms* ✧ THE MOON ✧ **A**
bit by Beatrix Potter, **Alice's Adventures in Wonderland** *by Lewis Carroll*, **Great Expectations** *by Charles Dickens*, **Adventures of Huckleberry Finn** *by Mark Twain*, **A Christmas Carol** *by Charles Dickens*, **Moby Dick** *by Herma*
EA ✧ **The Voyages of Doctor Dolittle** *by Hugh Lofting*, **The Swiss Family Robinson** *by Johann David Wyss*, **Robinson Crusoe** *by Daniel Defoe*, **The Count of Monte Cristo** *by Alexandre Dumas*, **Kidnapped** *by Robert Louis Ste*
ntures of Pinocchio by Carlo Collodi and **Twenty Thousand Leagues Under the Sea** *by Jules Verne* ✧ THE HOLE ✧ **Alice's Adventures in Wonderland** *by Lewis Carroll* ✧ THE MOUNTAINS ✧ **Peter Pan and Wendy** *by J.M*
he Golden Goose as told by Jacob Grimm and Wilhelm Grimm, **Tom Thumb** *as told by Richard Johnson*, **The Golden Bird** *as told by Jacob Grimm and Wilhelm Grimm*, **Snow White and Rose Red** *as told by Jacob Grimm and Will*
y Bram Stoker ✧ THE ROPE ✧ **Rapunzel** *as told by Jacob Grimm and Wilhelm Grimm* ✧ THE CLOUDS ✧ **Suo Gân** *as adapted by Robert Bryan*, **Twinkle, Twinkle, Little Star** *by Jane Taylor*, **Hush-a-Bye Baby** *as adapted by Jo*
y Alcott, **The Three Musketeers** *by Alexandre Dumas*, **The Tale of Peter Rabbit** *by Beatrix Potter*, **Alice's Adventures in Wonderland** *by Lewis Carroll*, **Great Expectations** *by Charles Dickens*, **Adventures of Huckleberry Finn** *by*
alory and Sir James Knowles and **Rip Van Winkle** *by Washington Irving* ✧ THE SEA ✧ **The Voyages of Doctor Dolittle** *by Hugh Lofting*, **The Swiss Family Robinson** *by Johann David Wyss*, **Robinson Crusoe** *by Daniel Defoe, T*
Crusoe by Daniel Defoe, **The Swiss Family Robinson** *by Johann David Wyss*, **The Adventures of Pinocchio** *by Carlo Collodi* and **Twenty Thousand Leagues Under the Sea** *by Jules Verne* ✧ THE HOLE ✧ **Alice's Adventures**
nm and Wilhelm Grimm, **Hansel & Gretel** *as told by Jacob Grimm and Wilhelm Grimm*, **The Golden Goose** *as told by Jacob Grimm and Wilhelm Grimm*, **Tom Thumb** *as told by Richard Johnson*, **The Golden Bird** *as told by Jacob*
nd of Sleepy Hollow by Washington Irving, **Frankenstein** *by Mary Shelley* and **Dracula** *by Bram Stoker* ✧ THE ROPE ✧ **Rapunzel** *as told by Jacob Grimm and Wilhelm Grimm* ✧ THE CLOUDS ✧ **Suo Gân** *as adapted by Rober*
k Baum, **The Wind in the Willows** *by Kenneth Grahame*, **Little Women** *by Louisa May Alcott*, **The Three Musketeers** *by Alexandre Dumas*, **The Tale of Peter Rabbit** *by Beatrix Potter*, **Alice's Adventures in Wonderland** *by Lewis*
auty by Anna Sewell, **The Legends of King Arthur and His Knights** *by Sir Thomas Malory and Sir James Knowles and* **Rip Van Winkle** *by Washington Irving* ✧ THE SEA ✧ **The Voyages of Doctor Dolittle** *by Hugh Lofting*, **The**
Sea by Jules Verne ✧ THE WAVE ✧ **Gulliver's Travels** *by Jonathan Swift*, **Robinson Crusoe** *by Daniel Defoe*, **The Swiss Family Robinson** *by Johann David Wyss*, **The Adventures of Pinocchio** *by Carlo Collodi* and **Twenty Tho**
d by Robert Louis Stevenson ✧ THE FOREST ✧ **Little Red Cap** *as told by Jacob Grimm and Wilhelm Grimm*, **Hansel & Gretel** *as told by Jacob Grimm and Wilhelm Grimm*, **The Golden Goose** *as told by Jacob Grimm and Wilhel*
nzel as told by Jacob Grimm and Wilhelm Grimm ✧ THE MONSTER ✧ **The Legend of Sleepy Hollow** *by Washington Irving*, **Frankenstein** *by Mary Shelley* and **Dracula** *by Bram Stoker* ✧ THE ROPE ✧ **Rapunzel** *as told by Jac*
he Moon by Jules Verne ✧ THE WORLD ✧ **The Wonderful Wizard of Oz** *by L. Frank Baum*, **The Wind in the Willows** *by Kenneth Grahame*, **Little Women** *by Louisa May Alcott*, **The Three Musketeers** *by Alexandre Dumas,* **T**
he Secret Garden by Frances Hodgson Burnett, **Heidi** *by Johanna Spyri*, **Black Beauty** *by Anna Sewell*, **The Legends of King Arthur and His Knights** *by Sir Thomas Malory and Sir James Knowles and* **Rip Van Winkle** *by Washing*
Gulliver's Travels *by Jonathan Swift* and **Twenty Thousand Leagues Under the Sea** *by Jules Verne* ✧ THE WAVE ✧ **Gulliver's Travels** *by Jonathan Swift*, **Robinson Crusoe** *by Daniel Defoe*, **The Swiss Family Robinson** *by Joha*
✧ THE CAVE ✧ **Treasure Island** *by Robert Louis Stevenson* and **Kidnapped** *by Robert Louis Stevenson* ✧ THE FOREST ✧ **Little Red Cap** *as told by Jacob Grimm and Wilhelm Grimm*, **Hansel & Gretel** *as told by Jacob Grimm*
Grimm, **Beauty and the Beast** *by Jeanne-Marie Leprince de Beaumont* and **Rapunzel** *as told by Jacob Grimm and Wilhelm Grimm* ✧ THE MONSTER ✧ **The Legend of Sleepy Hollow** *by Washington Irving*, **Frankenstein** *by Mary*
ery and **Brahms' Lullaby** *by Johannes Brahms* ✧ THE MOON ✧ **Around the Moon** *by Jules Verne* ✧ THE WORLD ✧ **The Wonderful Wizard of Oz** *by L. Frank Baum*, **The Wind in the Willows** *by Kenneth Grahame*, **Little**
in, **A Christmas Carol** *by Charles Dickens*, **Moby Dick** *by Herman Melville*, **The Secret Garden** *by Frances Hodgson Burnett*, **Heidi** *by Johanna Spyri*, **Black Beauty** *by Anna Sewell*, **The Legends of King Arthur and His Knights**
Monte Cristo by Alexandre Dumas, **Kidnapped** *by Robert Louis Stevenson*, **Gulliver's Travels** *by Jonathan Swift* and **Twenty Thousand Leagues Under the Sea** *by Jules Verne* ✧ THE WAVE ✧ **Gulliver's Travels** *by Jonathan Swift*
nd by Lewis Carroll ✧ THE MOUNTAINS ✧ **Peter Pan and Wendy** *by J.M. Barrie* ✧ THE CAVE ✧ **Treasure Island** *by Robert Louis Stevenson* and **Kidnapped** *by Robert Louis Stevenson* ✧ THE FOREST ✧ **Little Red Cap** *as*
d Wilhelm Grimm, **Snow White and Rose Red** *as told by Jacob Grimm and Wilhelm Grimm*, **Beauty and the Beast** *by Jeanne-Marie Leprince de Beaumont* and **Rapunzel** *as told by Jacob Grimm and Wilhelm Grimm* ✧ THE MON*
inkle, Twinkle, Little Star by Jane Taylor, **Hush-a-Bye Baby** *as adapted by John Newbery* and **Brahms' Lullaby** *by Johannes Brahms* ✧ THE MOON ✧ **Around the Moon** *by Jules Verne* ✧ THE WORLD ✧ **The Wonderful Wiza**
reat Expectations by Charles Dickens, **Adventures of Huckleberry Finn** *by Mark Twain*, **A Christmas Carol** *by Charles Dickens*, **Moby Dick** *by Herman Melville*, **The Secret Garden** *by Frances Hodgson Burnett*, **Heidi** *by Johanne*
ily Robinson by Johann David Wyss, **Robinson Crusoe** *by Daniel Defoe*, **The Count of Monte Cristo** *by Alexandre Dumas*, **Kidnapped** *by Robert Louis Stevenson*, **Gulliver's Travels** *by Jonathan Swift* and **Twenty Thousand Leag**
Under the Sea by Jules Verne ✧ THE HOLE ✧ **Alice's Adventures in Wonderland** *by Lewis Carroll* ✧ THE MOUNTAINS ✧ **Peter Pan and Wendy** *by J.M. Barrie* ✧ THE CAVE ✧ **Treasure Island** *by Robert Louis Stevenson*
mb as told by Richard Johnson, **The Golden Bird** *as told by Jacob Grimm and Wilhelm Grimm*, **Snow White and Rose Red** *as told by Jacob Grimm and Wilhelm Grimm*, **Beauty and the Beast** *by Jeanne-Marie Leprince de Beaumont*
lm Grimm ✧ THE CLOUDS ✧ **Suo Gân** *as adapted by Robert Bryan*, **Twinkle, Twinkle, Little Star** *by Jane Taylor*, **Hush-a-Bye Baby** *as adapted by John Newbery* and **Brahms' Lullaby** *by Johannes Brahms* ✧ THE MOON ✧ **A**
bit by Beatrix Potter, **Alice's Adventures in Wonderland** *by Lewis Carroll*, **Great Expectations** *by Charles Dickens*, **Adventures of Huckleberry Finn** *by Mark Twain*, **A Christmas Carol** *by Charles Dickens*, **Moby Dick** *by Herma*
EA ✧ **The Voyages of Doctor Dolittle** *by Hugh Lofting*, **The Swiss Family Robinson** *by Johann David Wyss*, **Robinson Crusoe** *by Daniel Defoe*, **The Count of Monte Cristo** *by Alexandre Dumas*, **Kidnapped** *by Robert Louis St*
ntures of Pinocchio by Carlo Collodi and **Twenty Thousand Leagues Under the Sea** *by Jules Verne* ✧ THE HOLE ✧ **Alice's Adventures in Wonderland** *by Lewis Carroll* ✧ THE MOUNTAINS ✧ **Peter Pan and Wendy** *by J.M.*